Tiny human protection agency

Tiny Human Protection Agency

Children's Novel

Written by: Megan Landman
Illustrated by: Andres Eben

Mwanaka Media and Publishing Pvt Ltd,
Chitungwiza Zimbabwe
*
Creativity, Wisdom and Beauty

Publisher:

Mmap

Mwanaka Media and Publishing Pvt Ltd

24 Svosve Road, Zengeza 1

Chitungwiza Zimbabwe

mwanaka@yahoo.com

https//mwanakamediaandpublishing.weebly.com

Distributed in and outside N. America by African Books Collective

orders@africanbookscollective.com

www.africanbookscollective.com

ISBN: 978-0-7974-8619-5

EAN: 9780797486195

© Megan Landman 2018

Acknowledgements

This book is dedicated to my daily angels. Without my angels, I would not have lived the amazing life that I have lived thus far. To my father, my brothers, and anyone who has taken the time to love me, thank you. Always remember that tiny humans need to be loved and protected.

Mr. Richards Journey

Mr. Richards Journey

01

Do you like ice cream?

Smack! The ruler came crashing down onto the desk and every child in the classroom jumped to attention. Mr Richards was in a foul mood again and the class was praying for the bell to sound. No one wanted to be the target of one of Mr Richards' bad moods.

Most people wondered why he even became a teacher if he hated children so much. The only time he ever seemed to smile was when someone did something wrong in the classroom. The corners of his mouth would rise ever so slightly as he now had a reason to unleash his fury.

Today it was a little girl named Sally who set him off. The class was busy writing out lines:

I shall not disobey Mr Richards.
I shall not disobey Mr Richards.

As they obediently wrote out the lines, Mr Richards noticed little Sally passing a note to one of her friends. That's when the ruler came crashing down. Little Sally went bright red and froze in her seat. Mr Richards slowly made his way over to her and began to reprimand her.

"So, Sally…" he said, as he stepped forward. Sally's heart was racing. "… This is how you choose to disrespect me today?" Sally mumbled "I … I … I'm sorry, Sir."

"You are sorry?" he roared. "You insolent little critter, I will show you sorry!"

Mr Richards moved to the front of the classroom and addressed the class:

"Attention everyone, because of Sally's behaviour today you will all stay after school for an extra thirty minutes and complete your lines, 100 times!"

A groan came from the class and people began to glare at Sally.

The school bell rang and disappointment set in as the children continued to write out their lines.

Mr Richards continued: "You can all thank Sally later."

A tear rolled down Sally's face as she continued writing out her lines. Mr Richards moved back to his desk to grade papers, just another one of the chores he hated so much. As he was doing so, a rather peculiar man walked into his classroom. This man was strangely hypnotic and there was a great sense of power about him. He was dressed in suit pants, a bright white shirt, and a waist coat, but he was wearing sandals.

He was calm and confident and he was casually eating an ice cream sundae. A big ice cream sundae, in a big glass. He leant against the back wall of the classroom and said, "Mr Richards, do you like ice cream?"

Mr Richards was startled.

"Excuse me, who are you? If you are a parent of one of my students, then it is best that you make an appointment or wait for 30 minutes as the class is being punished," Mr Richards responded with his normal air of arrogance.

He noticed something else that was peculiar. None of the children in the class had turned to look at the man and it was almost as if they weren't moving. However there was no time to think about it because the peculiar man responded:

"No Sir, I am not one of your students' parents but believe me when I say that I have your students' best interests at heart. And you should also believe me when I say that it is in your best interests to give me a few moments of your time, good sir." The strange man spoke in such a way that Mr Richards could not ignore him.

"Alright, I will give you but a few moments of my time. How can I help you?"

"You could start by answering my question. Do you like ice cream?"

"Not particularly, why?"

"That doesn't surprise me in the least. The ice cream is spectacular. Look at it: it has hazelnuts, chocolate sauce, candied cherries and sprinkles and all those wondrous things all covering a rocky road ice cream. It's an explosion of flavour in your mouth and people say that they can't quite pinpoint the individual flavours but when they are all wrapped together, they make a taste sensation that fills you with happiness. Well, so I am told."

Mr Richards was completely baffled. This peculiar man stood there describing his ice cream in the most peculiar way. He had no idea what any of it had to do with him and he was growing more and more impatient.

"And so?" he retorted, "What does this have to do with me and what do you mean 'so you've been told'?"

"I cannot taste ice cream, Sir. But I can feel how it makes a child feel when they eat it."

Mr Richards was now incredibly irritated and all he could think was that this man was insane.

"I think its best that you leave." He went to open the door and as he did so the door slammed shut and his chair flew at him and forced him to sit down. He was too stunned to say anything; he stared with awe and fear at the peculiar man in front of him.

That is when he knew that his initial thoughts about the children were correct. They were completely frozen in time. Mr Richards couldn't believe what he was seeing.

He would never admit it out loud, but he was afraid.

"Let me introduce myself. My name is Raguel and I'm an angel." He took another spoonful of his ice cream and a cheeky smile crossed his face as he continued: "To be honest I am kind of a big deal. I'm like a boss angel; I oversee a really special group of angels called the Tiny Humans Protection Agency.

"I have an amazing team of 12 angels who report directly to me. Each of these twelve angels is the guardian of children who were born in a specific month. Our task is to watch over children, comfort them, and guide them. Our role is not to save a child; we cannot directly interfere in their lives. Some children are finely tuned to us and they will follow our lead, whereas others are not. Humans often refer to it as 'following their gut' or 'following their heart'".

"Is this some sort of joke?" Mr Richards asked feebly.

"Not at all, there is nothing funny about anything my team does." Raguel took the last bite of his ice cream and continued, "I like eating ice cream just to pretend that I can taste it. I often eat ice cream at a very specific time of day. I want to show you something, Mr Richards."

Raguel moved towards Mr Richards and wrapped his wings around him. As he did so the classroom began to spin and everything became blurry. Mr Richards felt nauseous; it felt like sea sickness mixed with bad food poisoning. Within seconds he was transported miles away out of his classroom.

Everything stopped spinning but Mr Richards was too afraid to open his eyes. Raguel no longer had his wings wrapped around him but poked him as he said, "Come on then, open your eyes." When he opened his eyes, things started to come into focus. They were sitting on top of a building that Mr Richards didn't know.

Raguel was sitting next to him. He remained cool and calm and he continued "Sir, this is the favourite part of my day and it happens all over the world, just at different times. This is the time of day that I eat an ice cream, because I imagine that what I feel now is what it feels like when a child eats an ice cream sundae. Wait for it...5, 4, 3, 2, 1."

Briiiinnng briiiinnng!

Below them a school bell began to ring and the school children flooded out of the gates. Something odd was happening inside Mr Richards. It was as if Raguel had tethered their souls together and all of Raguel's emotions were being channelled through him. He was feeling a mix of joy, happiness, relief, and excitement! He couldn't contain himself, and he began to smile. A genuine smile.

"You see Mr Richards, every day I sit on top of a school and let all these happy emotions wash over me. For me it's just like that ice cream sundae. Once I know that they are all safe, I can fly off to continue my job. But today was different. Today I chose to sit on top of your school and instead of experiencing the joy of it all, do you know what I felt instead?"

Mr Richards was still feeling the effects of the happiness that surrounded him, but then the coldness of his day filled him, and he remembered little Sally. He knew what the angel was going to say, so he chose to remain silent.

"I felt fear and sadness today, Mr Richards. As I sat on the rooftop of your school, I felt the happiness of all the other children as they were let out of school but the strange thing was that it wasn't the strongest emotion that I felt. The strongest emotion that I felt was emanating from a corner of the school, your corner. The normal spark that lives within a child was not in the children of your class and it was all because of you…"

As Mr Richards absorbed the words, the world began to spin again and instantly he was back in his classroom.

02
Meeting
The Team

It took Mr Richards a few minutes to absorb everything. They sat in silence, staring at each other. Finally, Mr Richards stood up and began pacing the classroom. He was angry and confused. He believed this was all a dream, but he was stubborn. He wasn't going to let anyone get the better of him, even if it turned out to be in his own dream.

"And so what if the children were fearful and a bit sad?" he snapped at Raguel.

"Are you so blind and angry that you cannot see what is before you? Tiny humans are the future; they are the source of everything pure and happy in the world. Can you not see that, Sir?"

Before Mr Richards had a chance to speak, he heard harps playing. He thought for certain that he was going crazy now. Raguel pulled out a small device and said, "Excuse me sir, but I have an urgent call."

He pressed a button on the device and a hologram appeared in front of them. The hologram began to speak. "Raguel, what's wrong? Why have you called an urgent gathering?"

"Nothing's wrong, Azzie, please just send out a message on WingRing and get the group together at the following location. I will need your help on a special project."

"All right boss, we are on it."

"Who was that?" Mr Richards asked.

"One of the other angels on my team. Let me tell you more about us before they all get here…"

Mr Richards was nervous. Who was coming? Why were they coming? All he wanted was to be left alone. Those snotty children were enough to deal with, and now he thought he was going crazy. However he couldn't budge. He felt as if he was trapped in his classroom by an unknown force. He could only watch and listen – he didn't seem to have a choice.

Suddenly all the blinds in the classroom closed and the lights went out. Another hologram appeared, and Raguel began to speak: "Our angels are specifically created to help in every situation in a child's life. As you will notice when I introduce you to the team, our angels are younger and trendier than humans would think. As you humans change your trends, so do we. However, there are some basic things that never change about our angels. This is what one of our angels looks like:

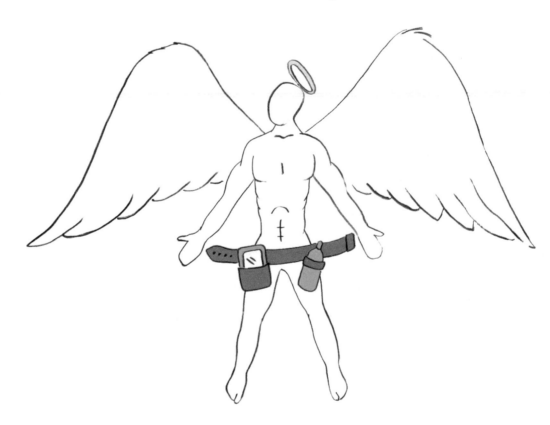

"Our wings are super soft and warm; these help when a child needs to be comforted. The wings are not fragile, they are bullet proof; this is for protection, even against the harshest of words.

Our halos are our GPS system. They can hear the faintest of whimpers and the tiniest cry for help. It can hear a tear falling. In tough situations we have a can of Calmeeze. This is made from the freshest water. It comes directly from a cloud. We have a choir of angels who can be compared to scientists on earth. They take the water and they add a pinch of laughter, a tablespoon of happiness, 2 table spoons of tranquillity, and a pinch of love (love is very potent, if they added in more it would become more like a love potion). They mix it all together and it creates this bottle of spray.

Each angel also has an aPad. This is where they keep their journals, and their files on every child they look after. They can also access WingRing on it; this is the angel's version of Facebook."

"So, as you can see, Mr Richards, we are no fly by night organisation! We are strong and we are needed."

"That's beautiful," Mr Richards said, the sarcasm in his tone unmistakeable, "but what does any of this have to do with me? If it has to do with Sally today then you are wrong. She had it coming. That disrespectful child deserved to be reminded of her place in the world, that snotty little…"

"That's enough!" roared Raguel, extending his wings to their full capacity. Mr Richards went quiet and turned a ghostly white.

"You are a very clever man, Mr Richards, and I agree with you, children have a place in this world, but it is you, Sir, who needs the reminding."

Raguel turned to his aPad again and a new hologram appeared. It looked like a map of the world; it had 12 different little sets of angel wings scattered around the globe. Each set of wings showed Raguel the location of each of his angels; it had their minutes till arrival and a status underneath it.

10 minutes away and Gabby writes: #runninglate #forgivenessisreal

At work and Barchiel says:
Punctuality should have been in the commandments.

Mackey-D 2 minutes away:
"Yo, what a beautiful morning!"

Azzie, 1 minute away
Wooosah, traffic is a good thing! It means that angels are doing their work!

Amy at work:
This is my 17th update of the morning! Guess what? I am at work and ready to go, go, go, go! Where did I put my coffee?

"Sir, when my angels get here, I require you to be silent. There is protocol that must be followed when we gather. You, Sir, are our guest but you are to be a polite guest and wait your turn."

Mr Richards meekly nodded; it was all he could muster now. Raguel sent out a message on his aPad; it read: "I am ready for you now, here is my location."

Within seconds there was a flash of white light, like lightning, it filled the classroom. It was warm and welcoming. Instantly the room was filled with 12 other peculiar beings. Mr Richards tried to take it all in.

The 13 angels gathered in a circle; they were ever so quiet. They wrapped their wings around each other and bowed their heads. A voice began to speak, but it was more like singing – soft but strong and almost all knowing. Mr Richards recognised it as Raguel's voice. They were chanting:

Are you Cherubim, the ones who proclaim defence of the little people?
Yes, yes, yes we are!
Are you their choir whose voices carry only messages of love?
Yes, yes, yes we are!
Every day will you strive to comfort and protect? Will you do so with passion and conviction?
Yes, yes, yes we will!

Angels, make your pledge:

To you our little ones, we promise to put a smile on your faces,
We will be your light in the darkest of spaces,
We will be your warmth on the coldest of days,
We will guide you through any maze
And through it all, we wish only to be your friend.
On us you can always depend.
To you our little ones, this is our solemn promise.

The bright light faded and they untangled themselves from their circle. They suddenly became more humanlike. Raguel continued:

"Thank you for coming on such short notice. I know that we are all very busy but I need your help. Everyone, this is Mr Richards, he is a teacher at this school and I would like us to share some stories with him."

Mr Richards heard a few greetings. "Good day, Sir" said one. "What's up, Mr R?" said another. "Nice to meet you!" sang one. The angels were moving about the classroom. They were going to the children and hovering around them.

The angels noticed that Mr Richard's classroom was bleak. There were no signs of happiness anywhere. The desks were in orderly rows. The walls had nothing on them. Mr Richards kept only half of the lights on. It was cold and dreary. It sent shivers down their spines.

While the angels were examining the classroom, Mr Richards was examining them. He noticed that each angel was different; besides the basics that Raguel had shown in him the hologram. Each angel had a unique style. Mr Richards noticed that one angel looked particularly young; he was dressed like a skateboarder and he had scruffy blonde hair. He was standing next to a little boy named Ben, and he was talking to him…wait, he was in fact rapping!

Mr Richards saw another angel who was sitting on the desk of a girl named Emily. This angel was strikingly beautiful. She had long black hair with piercing blue eyes. She was tall and elegant and immaculately dressed. She was spraying some weird concoction over Emily. Mr Richards could only guess that it was the can of Calmeeze that Raguel had shown him earlier.

They were all so beautiful and majestic. Mr Richards was still weary of them, though. He continued to scan the room and when he looked at Sally's desk he noticed that her angel was behaving differently to the others. His focus was not entirely on Sally. He was standing behind Sally and his wings were wrapped around her. He was staring at Mr Richards. This angel was big. He looked like he was the tallest of all the angels and he was muscular. He was wearing a pair of tight-fitting jeans and a tight vest. He had on cowboy boots and Mr Richards knew that he meant business. He looked angry and would not stop staring at Mr Richards.

"Can I help you?" Mr Richards blurted out.

"Mr Richards!" shouted Raguel. "You were told not to speak until spoken to!"

"Yes, you can help me!" thundered the enormous angel. There wasn't even enough time to blink and the large angel was right in front of Mr Richards. All the other angels turned to see what was happening and Raguel was trying to diffuse the tension that had suddenly filled the room.

"Now Gabriel, calm down. We are here to help, not to fight." Raguel tried his best to get through to Gabriel, but he wasn't listening.

"Mr Richards, was it? Do you have any idea what you have done to little Sally over there?" Gabriel roared.

Mr Richards was to have none of this; he would defend himself whether he was right or wrong: "Yes I do. I punished her for bad behaviour. Don't you...you...whatever you are, don't you believe in rules?"

Gabriel was getting angrier. "We most certainly do! But we also believe in treating people with compassion and respect. Do you know what those words even mean, or should I find a dictionary for you?"

All the other angels were gathering around now. The angel who looked like a skateboarder had conjured up a bowl of popcorn and he was munching away as he watched the fight unfurl.

It wasn't to last long though as Raguel had had enough. He whistled loudly – a piercing sound that left everyone's ears ringing for minutes afterwards.

"That's enough! Everyone sit down. Gabriel, calm yourself. You will have your chance to speak. I would like you to activate the storyteller mode on your aPads."

All the angels pulled out their aPads and began pressing buttons. Raguel pulled out what looked like a set of goggles and said: "Alright then, let's take Mr Richards on a journey that he will never forget! Remember to activate the emotions emitter so that Mr Richards can feel everything in the story. Since Gabriel has so much to say, I will hand over the floor to him."

03
Sally's
Secret

Gabriel was still fuming, you could see his muscles flexing as he tried to control his emotions. He said to Mr Richards: "What exactly do you know about Sally?"

"Umm, she is a new girl at the school. She has been here a couple of weeks. Average student from what I can tell."

"That's all you know?"

"Yes, what else should I know?" Mr Richards was not impressed by being interrogated like this. "What business is it of yours what I know?"

Gabriel chuckled; it was an all-knowing chuckle. "Well you see, this is exactly my business. What day is it today, Mr Richards?"

"It's Monday, the 29th of January."

"Indeed it is. It is also little Sally's birthday and I am responsible for all children born in the month of January. This means that Sally is my business."

"Get on with it, Gabriel, this is not a competition. Mr Richards can see that you are big and strong. Tell us your story and stop provoking him!"

Gabriel was being hurried by a rather cute angel. She reminded Mr Richards of an art teacher. She was short and had one of the biggest afros Mr Richards had ever seen. He wondered how such a small body could support such a large amount of hair. She was wearing colourful baggy pants and Mr Richards would later find out that her name was Uriel. He felt drawn to her.

Gabriel got the message; standing up, he walked over to Mr Richards. He was carrying the set of goggles that Raguel had taken out earlier. Each angel then pulled out their own set of goggles and put them on.

The skateboarder angel asked, "Does anyone want some of my popcorn?" A few of the angels grabbed some popcorn and everyone settled down.

"Right," continued Gabriel, "now Mr Richards, we are going to go into a memory of little Sally's. She cannot hear us or see us. You cannot change anything in the memory, just enjoy the show."

Gabriel placed the goggles on Mr Richards' face. At first, all he could see was darkness; then he saw a small light in the distance, coming towards him. As it grew nearer, he noticed that it was Gabriel, holding a lantern. He reached out and took Mr Richards' hand. "Come with me, the others are already situated in the memory."

He took Gabriel's hand and followed him through the darkness. With each step they took, things began to come into focus. He noticed that he was standing in a garden. A house started to come into focus. All the other angels were close by, either sitting in a tree or on the grass.

"This is where little Sally lived a year ago. She lives with her mother. She has 2 sisters and a brother. She also lives with her mother's boyfriend who has two children of his own. They are a poor family and her mother's boyfriend moves around a lot for work. This is the fourth house that Sally has lived in, in one year. The school that she was in at this time was her third school that year."

Gabriel opened the front door and they walked in. Mr Richards noticed the time on a clock on the wall. It was very early in the morning.

They heard some movement coming from the kitchen. Sally's mother was in there lighting some candles on a birthday cake.

"Today is also Sally's birthday," Gabriel said.

They watched Sally's mother quietly go and wake up the other children. Gabriel and Mr Richards made their way into Sally's room. She shared the room with her sister. They watched her for a while. Something strange began to happen to Mr Richards.

As he looked at her, he began to feel what she was feeling. She was secretly awake and the most immense excitement filled her.

She knew what was about to happen. She could barely contain herself but she was pretending to be asleep. Mr Richards was so excited that he started to look for what was coming her way.

Suddenly, the darkness of the room was filled with candlelight and the voices of her family rang throughout the house: "Happy birthday to you! Happy birthday to you! Happy birthday dear Sally, happy birthday to you!"

The family sang in unison as Sally sat up in her bed with the biggest smile. Mr Richards was also smiling. He felt like it was his birthday, and the love that filled the room filled him too.

They watched as Sally was kissed by her mother, and the other family members said happy birthday. All the kids started to pile onto the bed. It was so warm and comfortable. Sally's mother said: "Get the knife; it's time for cake for breakfast!" "Yay!" shouted most of the children as they prepared themselves for a slice of chocolate heaven.

Gabriel touchéd Mr Richards arm and said, "Every year the children get to choose a birthday present. They know that it can't cost a lot of money but their parents do the best that they can.

"For this birthday, Sally asked her parents if she could have a birthday party instead of a gift. So that's where we are headed today, to Sally's birthday party."

The cake didn't take long to finish, and Sally's mother said: "Alright everyone, to your battle stations. I want everyone washed and ready in 30 minutes. I will also need help packing the car."

All the children were so excited. Birthday parties were the best! Sally was still in her bed and Mr Richards could tell that she felt so excited but she was also a little bit nervous. He didn't know why. The house became chaos within minutes.

Children were running about shouting at each other: "David! Where did you put the Frisbee?"
"It won't fall on your head, Matthew- just look
for it" "Found it!"

A shriek came from the other corner of the house:

"Mom! Where are my pink socks? Did you even wash them?"

Sally quietly closed her door and began to get ready. Her mother had taken her shopping the day before for new clothes. She got a pair of black pants, a t-shirt, and some really cool black sneakers. She felt so proud and loved as she got ready. Mr Richards hadn't felt emotion like this in a while. He had forgotten what family meant.

The family was ready, the car was packed and they left the house to go to the party. Everything started to become dark again and Mr Richards noticed the lantern in front of him again. Gabriel took his hand and said, "Come on; let's go to the next part of her memory."

Everything started coming into focus again; they were in a very beautiful park. Mr Richards saw Sally's parents setting up a table. It was full of treats. A sugar festival! All of Sally's siblings were running around the park having a blast but Sally sat by herself under a tree and waited.

Gabriel motioned to Mr Richards and they joined Sally under the tree. Her emotions were so strong; she was worried. She was tapping her foot and she kept checking the time. Gabriel said: "Sally had only been at the school for 2 weeks when she decided to have the party. Her mother had suggested that they invite everyone in the class. The invitation said that the party would start at 11h00. It is now 11h10 and Sally's worst nightmare is about to come true."

Sally went to talk to her mother. She was moving slowly. The world had disappointed her. She sat next to her mother and said, "What if they don't come?"

"Give it some more time, they will come. And if they don't then you don't want friends like them."

At that moment, no words would help Sally. It would take her years to realise that her mother was right. But right then and there, she just wanted to have a fun-filled day.

Time kept ticking by and Sally was growing sadder by the minute. Mr Richards could feel everything that she was feeling. He was so angry, his thoughts echoed hers: how could they not come! It's a birthday party. How will she cope at school after this? How could people be so mean?

At 12 o'clock there was still no one at the party and Sally decided that she was going to hide in a tree. Gabriel and Mr Richards followed her. Gabriel told Mr Richards that it was at times like this that an angel is needed. He explained that he would use the Calmeeze in a situation like this and he would whisper happier thoughts or solutions to her problem.

What did you tell her?" Asked Mr Richards.

"Well, I was busy telling her that true friends would come her way. I was telling her that this pain would make her stronger and that she had the love of her family to comfort her.

Mr Richards, one of our favourite things to witness as angels is the influence that other humans have on each other. There are several daily angels that help us. Today this little daily angel took the form of her little brother, David. He was a cute kid; he had striking blonde locks and he was one of her best friends. David climbed the tree and helped me. Watch what happened…"

Mr Richards saw a little kid climbing the tree. The boy sat next to Sally on her branch, and said, "I'm sorry, Sally. Those kids are stupid."

Sally began to cry. David held her hand. "Come on," he said, "we have a game of Frisbee going and I bet we can win! I will even give you my hotdog today if you want."

Sally started to smile and Gabriel continued: "It only took this simple act of kindness to warm her soul. She knew how much David loved hotdogs. Sally was still hurt but she followed her brother, her daily angel, and went to play."

Everything went dark again. Mr Richards heard Gabriel instruct him to take off the goggles. They were back in the classroom.

Some angels were drying the tears from their eyes. Mr Richards was not sure what he felt. Gabriel had taken him on a rollercoaster of emotions. He looked at Sally and felt closer to her.

"Today, when Sally was sending a note to one of her friends, it was to confirm that she could spend the weekend with her to celebrate her birthday. The whole day today, Sally was filled with dread because she would never forget how she felt that day."

"I didn't realise," Mr Richards said feebly.

"Of course you didn't!" Gabriel raised his voice slightly.

The strikingly beautiful angel stood up and went to kiss Sally on her forehead. She turned to Gabriel and thanked him for the story. She continued:

"I just love it when other humans become angels. We cannot do it all you know. I have a story about another human angel. Raguel, would you mind if I went next?"

Gabriel sat down, but he was still glaring at Mr Richards. He was unsure that he the teacher had really understood. He reluctantly gave the goggles to the beautiful angel.

"It's all yours, Amy."

04

Emily's Dilemma

"Good day, Mr Richards, my name is Amy." She walked over to Mr Richards and kissed him on each cheek. He went bright red but greeted her back. She was so well dressed and beautiful. She continued:

"My job is to look after the children born in the month of May, but my passion is fashion. Oh my, how I have loved fashion through the years. It all started one day a few centuries ago when I started comparing the clothes that different cultures wore.

Now I find myself watching Fashion TV, reading the humans' magazines on fashion and going to as many fashion shows as I can in my spare time."

Two angels began to giggle. Amy turned to look at them: "What?"

"Nothing," said an angel named Azzie "We just had a friendly wager. I told Vee that you would tell us a story about fashion and well … there you go."

"Very funny you two! I can't help it that I love fashion. You see, Mr Richards," she continued, completely ignoring the other two, "clothes have become a very important part of a human's existence.

"As the tiny humans grow up, it begins to play a very important role in their lives. Their self-esteem is somehow connected to these garments. One of my fascinations lies with the clothes that they deem to be a necessity. One such garment is called a 'brassier' or 'bra' for short."

There were more giggles from the angels; this time it was the skateboarder. Amy quickly turned to him and said, "Oh come on, grow up Mackey!"

"Ok, ok, go on. I'm sorry." He was still giggling as he said this. Amy sighed and continued, "It is something that women seem to think that they need to wear and when they reach a certain age, they start wearing it."

Mackey couldn't contain his laughter, and Amy was getting annoyed. Mr Richards was starting to enjoy this. Raguel stood up and said, "Enough! Get on with it."

"I'm trying to," Amy said, as she stood to walk towards a girl sitting in the back of the classroom. She was dressed in shorts, sneakers and a t-shirt. "Mr Richards, do you know this girl?"

"Yes, of course, her name is Emily Wright. Before you ask, I only know that she loves sports and isn't very academically inclined."

"Well, Mr Richards, kudos to you. You are right. What you perhaps don't know is that Emily's life so far has been an interesting one. She lives with her three brothers and her father.

Her mother and father divorced when she was six years old. Her mother moved to another country. Emily misses her mother a lot. Talking on the phone and visiting her every two years never really satisfies her need for a mother. Emily is what is termed a 'tomboy'. Tomboys are girls that love to do the things that boys are supposed to do, and they love to wear the clothes that boys love to wear. So, Emily's favourite day consists of playing sport with her brothers, climbing along the walls of her neighbourhood, and running around outside in the sun.

"I happened on this story by mistake. You see, I was already at Emily's house. Her younger brother had been going through a pretty rough time. He had been wetting his bed at night, and whenever he woke up he felt immense shame and was constantly confused by what he had done. I was there to comfort him and to try make him realise that there was no shame in what had happened. Let's go have a look."

Amy walked over to Mr Richards and placed the goggles on him. In the darkness he found Amy and followed her. When everything came into focus, Mr Richards could see that they were in a house. A small boy was lying on the sofa, watching TV. Mr Richards could hear music coming from a room down the passage and he could hear someone cooking in the kitchen.

"I was sitting with her little brother when I saw Emily emerge from her bedroom and go to the kitchen where her father was busy preparing toast and tea for everyone."

Mr Richards moved into the kitchen. He saw her father look up at his little girl and jokingly say, "Oooh the breast fairy visited you last night." Her emotions skyrocketed. Mr Richards was taken aback! He was feeling everything that she was. Amy came over to Mr Richards and held out a device called an emotionsograph. Mr Richards could see that there was a drastic rise in her emotions.

Mr Richards moved even closer to listen; besides, he thought her father was funny. Emily was feeling panicked and slightly annoyed at her father's flippant use of humour in a situation like this. She didn't fully understand what was happening; she didn't know why her body was changing and who this breast fairy was.

Her father explained to her that she was at the age where her body was changing and that perhaps it was time for them to look at getting her the right clothes to make her more comfortable. She was still annoyed:

"What clothes?" she snapped.

He calmly replied, "You know, a training…"

Time seemed to slow down here for Emily because she had been dreading this moment. In a split second all her favourite memories of running around outside with no shirt on and being free raced through her mind.

"….bra".

She had a look of disappointment on her face. Her father noticed it and said: "Come on, we can make a day of it. Just you and I." She stood up and went to her bedroom to sulk; she was worried. A thought crossed her mind: what does my dad know about buying bras?

Everything went black again and when things came into focus, Mr Richards saw that they were now in a department store. He looked around and was slightly amused. All the other angels were spread out around the store. He saw Gabriel trying on some hats, the cute one, Uriel, was trying on some sunglasses. One of them was sitting on a chair in the shoe section, reading a newspaper.

"Oh, come on, everyone!" Amy shouted. "Gather round"
The angels made their way over and Amy continued.

"The next Saturday she headed to the shops with her dad. I had diarised it because I thought that this situation could be humorous and besides, I wanted to try and give her a little guidance. I wanted her to know that change isn't a bad thing and that her father wasn't trying to punish her in anyway. Also, they were going shopping for clothes, my favourite thing. Her father took her to her favourite restaurant for breakfast and then they headed off to the clothes shop."

Everyone turned to look, and they saw Emily and her father. They moved slowly past the women's work-wear department. As they walked through the store, Mr Richards could feel Emily growing more and more anxious.

Her father was in a world of his own; he was not sure what was about to happen. He hadn't really thought this through yet. And then there it was … the women's underwear department. They stood hand in hand and surveyed the landscape before them. They had no idea where to start. There were big ones, small ones, fancy ones, enormous ones, pink ones, some in packs of two or three and some all by themselves. Father and daughter stood there in complete silence – like two deer's caught in headlights.

Mr Richards noticed that Amy was now besides Emily. She hugged her and then flew off to find some help. She saw a woman buying a bra a few aisles down and whispered a request in her ear. The woman started to walk towards them. Emily's father said, "Umm, let's …" followed by a nervous pause "err, ok, why don't you …" Another nervous pause.

Just then a woman looked up and noticed the confusion. She walked over and said:
"The bras for young ladies are over there."
"Oh, thank you very much," her father replied.
Emily went bright red.
"Why don't I give her a hand?" the lady offered.
"Yes, yes, that would be great!" her father replied.

Everything went black again, until Mr Richards found himself in the car with Emily and her father. Their shopping was complete, and Emily was contemplating her fate as her dad said to her, "You know, Em, buying this bra doesn't mean you have to change who you are. It just means that you will be wearing something different.

"You can still play outside, and you can still play with all of your friends. You can still play sports and climb up walls. You are perfect, and I don't want you to change. This silly piece of clothing is only meant to help you feel more comfortable. Wear it with pride, my growing girl!"

When Emily got home, she hugged her dad and ran to her room to put on her new bra and her dirty old t-shirt.

Mr Richards sat in the living room and he could feel that Emily was once again at peace.

As Emily headed outside to play, Amy lay next to Emily's little brother on the sofa to watch TV. She turned to Mr Richards and said: "I was happy in the thought that there are angels all around us. Angels who can help in even the most trivial of situations."

Before Mr Richards knew it, he was back in the classroom. He sat in silence and thought about everything he had seen so far. He looked at Emily, and understood her just a little bit more.

05

Double
Trouble

"Right on little Emily!" the skateboarder angel stood up and clapped. "I love it when children grow up a little. It's even better when the big humans help them out. What ya think, Mr R?"

"Umm, I don't really know." Mr Richards knew what he should say but he truly didn't understand.

Raguel chimed in, "You are right, Mackey, but I've noticed that some of the best stories come from when children help each other. If I remember correctly, Mackey, you have a pretty good story about the twins in this class. Don't you?"

"I totally do!" Mackey jumped up and fixed his cap. He moved over to Mr Richards and fist-pumped him, "The name's Mackey-D, my official name is Machidiel but it's a bigger mouthful than the burger my nickname comes from. So, my list of children comprises some weird and wacky little kids but one day my radar took me to this awesome little brother and sister duo."

Mackey-D moved over to the brother and sister who were sitting in the front of the classroom." Mr R, I'm guessing you don't know much about them so I'm going to enlighten you and everyone else.

"They are twins, but he is shy, soft-spoken and smaller than the other boys their age. His hair is always perfectly brushed, and he is wicked smart. He loves sport and he can rattle off rules, strategies, and statistics in his sleep. He's a cute little guy; his name is Ben. His twin sister, Betty, is his polar opposite. She is loud and funny, so much so that my stomach hurts sometimes after listening to her ramble. Her hair is always a mess and she is very forgetful. She is also a small kid, but she is a bucket load more physically active than he is."

"Anyway, one day I was in their neighbourhood watching some kids at a skate park. If I didn't have wings I would totally buy a skateboard, awesome little inventions. You know, I knew the kid who invented the skateboard. I comforted him one day after his first invention failed – he tried to make roller-skates for his hands."

"Yes, yes," said a rather stern looking angel. He was the angel who had been reading the newspaper in the department store. "I was Albert Einstein's angel. Get on with it will you, Machadiel."

"Sorry Barchiel, you know I like to digress sometimes, that's a story for another time. Let's go check it out."

Mr Richards knew the drill by now and put the goggles on. Mackey-D led him to a skate park. Uriel and two other angels were giving skateboarding a go. Amy was standing as far away from them as she could. She even had protective sheets over her fancy high-heeled shoes.

"So, Mr R, as I was watching the skaters my halo began to vibrate. I was annoyed. I thought it was on silent; but then I started listening. A whole lot of emotions were at play somewhere nearby. I could feel fear, worthlessness, and anger but there was an overriding emotion of protectiveness. A pot of emotions like this was surely going to have an explosive end so I had to go and see what was brewing. I had to do something to calm the situation."

They walked down the road to find out what was happening. As they drew closer, Mr Richards could feel exactly what Mackey-D had picked up. This pot of emotions was volatile and Mr Richards was confused.

They arrived at the school sports fields and saw the twins surrounded by a group of slightly older and bigger kids. It seemed that some sort of fight was about to start.

Mackey-D motioned for Mr Richards to sit on the spectator stands close by so that he could watch. Mackey-D continued: "From what I could gather there had been a game of rugby just a few minutes earlier.

Ben had been allowed to play but he was instructed to get rid of the ball as soon as he got it. The one time the ball got to him, his knowledge of the sport kicked in and he tried to do something that he thought was right. Unfortunately, the poor little guy didn't have the necessary skill and got taken out by the bigger guys resulting in his team losing. It's his own team mates that are now picking on him. Betty had seen this all happen and ran to his side."

They continued to watch as the fight continued. As the group of boys flung insults at Ben, Mr Richards could feel his self-worth dwindling by the second. It was like watching a sparkler slowly fizzle out. Mackey-D had placed himself next to Ben and was whispering cool things about him into his ear. He was trying to keep the spark alive. Just then Mr Richards realised where the overwhelming feeling of protectiveness was coming from; it was Betty. When he looked at her she was radiating that emotion.

Mackey-D noticed that Mr Richards was looking at Betty. He said: "You know, Betty cannot control these strong emotions yet and she often acts quickly, I knew something was going to happen with her, but my place was with Ben now, his spark was fading. I had to let her act the best way she knew how, which wasn't necessarily very good at all today. "

One of the big boys said to Ben "You might as well have been a girl too, just like your sister!" That was the last straw; Betty had had enough. This was her brother; she could feel his distress and she was not going to have it. With all her might she kicked that boy so hard that the playground seemed to stand still.

There was a hush in the air; every tiny human stopped to look. Powered by her love for her brother she shouted, "This is my brother and you WILL leave him alone!" The bullies began to disperse as the meanest of the lot slumped to the floor and whimpered. Ben ran away. Betty was left confused.

Everything faded to black. Then Mr Richards found himself sitting in what could only have been a little boy's room. Toys and books were strewn all over the room. Ben came rushing into the room and slammed the door. He collapsed on his bed. Mackey-D sat beside him and said to Mr Richards:

"For the rest of the day Ben did not speak to Betty. He was so upset that he didn't even eat his fish fingers and mashed potato, which is his favourite."

Mackey-D made everything fade to black again but instead of returning to the classroom or to another memory, he and Mr Richards sat on what could only be described as a park bench in the darkness. It was cold and uninviting. Mackey-D continued, "Sometimes I sit here and reflect. It reminds me of the lonely and dark places that a tiny human's mind can take them. I reflect so that I know how to help them in the future, because there is always a way out of the darkness. I sat with Ben the whole night; I wrapped my wings around him and let him work through this. His mind was troubled. He loved his sister dearly, but she too had made him feel worthless. He felt like he couldn't stand up for himself.

He didn't understand how she could be so brave, so fearless and so driven by emotion and how he just stood there, frozen and unable to deal with those boys.

He fell asleep in my wings with tears rolling down his face. I spoke to him while he slept. Comforting words: 'This too shall pass, take comfort in your sister's love; words of strength: "You too are strong, my boy, your strength is just a different kind'. I told him that both love and hate are strong emotions and even though what his sister had done was not totally right it still came from a place of love and this he must try to understand."

The darkness started to fade and Mr Richards found himself in another bedroom; this time it was clearly a girl's room, albeit a very messy girl. Ben made his way into the room, where his sister lay fast asleep. Her head was on the wrong side of the bed and her pyjamas were mismatched. He went over to her and kissed her forehead gently and said, "I love you too."

Everything faded to black and as he followed Mackey-D back through the darkness and into the classroom, Mr Richards said to him:

"He found bits of his sparkle in his sister again."

06
Her
Animal
Shadow

Raguel had heard what Mr Richards had said and was glad that he was finally starting to see what the angels wanted him to see. However, he wasn't sure that the message had really sunk in yet. It was time to up the ante a bit and Raguel knew just the story to show Mr Richards how fragile yet strong tiny humans could be.

Everyone was sitting around chatting after Mackey-D's story. Raguel had brought in some donuts and tea.

Mr Richards had never tasted such an amazing donut before in his life. Every bit of it was perfect; even each grain of sugar tasted like it had come from the purest place in the world. He was curious and asked:

"I thought that you couldn't taste food?"

The angels laughed and nodded. Raguel said, "Oh we can't, we just love the act of eating. It makes us feel like we have something in common with the tiny humans."

"Why would you want that? Why get so emotionally involved?" Mr Richards asked nonchalantly.

"Well, Mr Richards, that's a very good question. Instead of answering, why don't we carry on with story time?"

The angels started to gather around. Some had been sitting next to the children and comforting them; they made their way over and took their seats.

Uriel said, "I'm so excited, I love story time! We all have so many but I just love to see what you all get up to." Her voice was soft and reassuring. Mr Richards thought he had heard it before.

"Agreed," said Raguel "Vee, are you ready to tell your story? I remember that there is a very special girl in this class who went through something recently that is pretty tough for a soft soul like hers. Do you remember which one I am talking about, Vee?"

Vee was one of the angels that had been giggling earlier during Amy's story. She was very energetic. She was dressed as though she just came from gym. She jumped to attention:

"Oh yes, I sure do!"

She stood up and moved over to a girl in the classroom. Mr Richards watched her as she went but he was still thinking about his perfect donut. His day-dream was interrupted by Vee addressing him:

"Mr Richards, my name is Vee and I am so totally 100 percent happy to share this story with you today. I am the angel for the month of July and wowee; I can't even explain how much I love all my children.

As the sun rises every day I do cartwheels to celebrate them. Afterwards I totally drink a smoothie to replace any electrolytes that I might have lost, I mean really, we angels are totally bodies of light, so I can't be losing any "lytes" in whatever form they take!"

She spoke at such a pace that it was hard to keep up with her, but she was mesmerizing at the same time.

"So, I have started blogging on WingRing about my children. You should totally check it out!" She was addressing the angels now. "After my story I will share it with all of you! Like and share it angels, like and share it! It is what makes WingRing work." She looked at Mr Richards now.

"Anyway, I write about the connection that children have with animals. I know that we have all shared stories about how another person can help a tiny human but I am fascinated by the relationship that tiny humans share with the furrier, smaller species. I brought some bottles of "Pure Lyte" for anyone who may shed a tear or two during my telling of this story." She handed out bottles of a very bright blue energy drink and said to Mr Richards, "Goggle up, let's go."

Vee led Mr Richards to a very cosy bedroom. The sun was just starting to come up. In the bed a girl lay sleeping. Mr Richards recognised her as Angela. She was a particularly bright student and well-behaved, so, naturally, Mr Richards had no problems with her. As long as the "little critters" stayed out of his hair and made him look good, then all was well with the world. She was ultimately just another name on the class list to tick off. Mr Richards heard a voice call out from somewhere in the house.

"Angela, get up! You only have 30 minutes to get ready for school and don't forget to feed Lilo before you leave!" It was Angela's mother. Angela slowly opened her eyes, and saw her cat, Lilo, staring at her. "Yes, Ma!" she shouted back, "between you and this fat cat, how could I forget?!" She scratched Lilos cute grey ears. "Come on fatso, let's go get some breakfast." Lilo followed closely behind her as she walked to the kitchen.

Mr Richards could feel the deep connection she had to her cat. He felt affection and he longed to pet the animal, but he resisted the temptation.

As he walked to the kitchen with Vee, she explained: "The cat was like this ever since she was a kitten; she was what I liked to call an animal shadow. They were best friends. No matter what Angela did, the fat cat was always around. She sat with her when she watched TV, she watched her do the dishes. She often waited outside the bathroom door when she took a bath.

She even hated homework as much as Angela does; the cat was constantly pushing her pens off of the desk or just rudely sitting right on top of her books My favourite though, was that she even walked Angela home after school. She would sit and wait on the wall at the end of the road and as Angela rounded the corner she meowed. It was almost as if you she said, 'Hey you, human! How was your day? Huh? Huh? Huh? Tell me, anything good happen? Let's walk and talk."

And they did; well, Angela did the talking and they both did the walking. You could feel the happiness rise up in the human every day as she rounded that corner, it was electric! You were the topic of conversation at times, Mr Richards." He ignored that comment because he was starting to understand that perhaps he didn't treat his students as well as he should.

That morning Angela was running late, and when she realized what time it was, she grabbed her school bag, quickly hugged her mom and said, "Bye Ma, see you a bit later!" Her mom squeezed her tightly. "Alright sweetie, please don't forget your rain jacket. The weather forecast says there will be a bad storm today." Angela grabbed her jacket and headed off to school, happy as a bee in honey.

Everything faded to black and when it all came back into focus; Mr Richards was standing at the corner of a road. The weather was atrocious. The wind was howling and dark clouds gathered above them.

Vee said: "My travels have taught me that moms are always right. A bit later that day the most incredible storm clouds came over and the winds picked up.

"A ferocious storm hit their city; it was almost as if the sky was at war with the earth. I am not sure who won that war but I know a lot of angels were about trying to help wherever they could. I was happy to see that the choir in charge of nature was doing what it could that day, strengthening roots, reassuring flowers and such."

Vee spoke to Mr Richards as the storm raged around them. Mr Richards looked around and Vee was right. He was surrounded by angels. They were battling the consequences of the storm. He saw angels talking to flowers. He saw some hugging trees. When he looked up at the sky, he saw a few angels shepherding some birds to safety.

The storm died down and they took in the destruction that it had caused. A few moments later, Angela came walking down the street. Mr Richards could feel what she was feeling as she walked along. He could feel her heart break as she noticed the wounds that the earth had suffered. Branches had been ripped from the trees and entire fields of grass were now swamps. As she neared the corner where her animal shadow normally waited, he could feel the anxiety build within her.

Mr Richards saw Vee whispering in her ear. "Keep going my child, it will be ok." The wall where the fat cat normally sat had been damaged by the storm. Angela thought: "Where would she wait for me now?" Lilo wasn't there and Angela began to call for her. "Lilo! My fatso, where are you?" She called for her the whole way home. There was no response.

Angela was in a state of despair. She felt sad and useless. Vee sat with her for most of the night, offering her some comfort. That night after she fell asleep and Mr Richards heard Vee whisper to her: "You can totally take action little one, turn your worry into energy and use it to look for your Lilo. Tomorrow you can knock on doors, you can put up posters and you can send positive energy out into the world. Perhaps Lilo will hear you, perhaps she will feel you."

The next morning, as Angela sat at the breakfast table she noticed Lilos' empty food bowl and this lonely sight motivated her to take action. Mr Richards followed her around as she spent the rest of the day putting up posters around the neighbourhood. Mr Richards was growing tired. All he could feel was Angela's anxiety and utter sadness.

Vee gave him a bit of a reprieve when she started talking to him. She told him that on that day she hugged Angela tightly and went off to chat to the choir in charge of nature.

When I arrived there, I chatted to a lovely angel. She was very helpful and comforting. But I am afraid she had bad news. Lilo had in fact not survived the storm. A wave of sadness washed over me and I thought 'Oh Angela, how can I help you now?'"

Mr Richards began to cry. How do you help her? He thought. Everything faded to black.

As Mr Richards was drying his eyes he heard Angela's mother shout: "Angela, get up! You only have 30 minutes to get ready for school." She heard her mother's voice, her morning wake up call. She had been awake for a while though. Vee told Mr Richards that it had been two weeks since the storm and Lilo was still on her mind. Her world was just not the same. She missed her shadow. With Lilo gone, her world felt dark.

"Mr Richards, a world without a shadow is a lonely place and one day I hope that her memory of her furry, fluffy and purring friend will cast enough light for her to find it again. But for now, I am her light. Every day I fly past her to help her grieve. A warm hug and a kiss on the forehead is the hope I give to her."

They left the memory in silence.

07
Waves of Happiness

Everyone in the classroom was quiet. A few sniffles were heard and Mackey-D was handing out tissues. For the first time that day, Mr Richards got up from his seat. He headed towards Vee.

Gabriel stood up protectively, he was still unsure of Mr Richards. But Mr Richards did something unexpected.

Mr Richards hugged Vee. It was the warmest hug that he had ever felt; he felt her strength and knew that she needed that type of strength to carry around the weight of all the children.

Although Raguel was moved, he had a cheeky smile on his face. He loved it when a plan came together.

"Oh, come on, guys," sniffled Uriel. "Can someone please lighten the mood, and no, Vee, I don't need more electrolytes. We live in such a happy and beautiful world. Let's show Mr Richards that too."

A very tanned angel stood up just then and searched the classroom. He said, "I think I have the perfect story!"

He moved over to a boy sitting in the back of the classroom. He sat next to the boy and pulled out his aPad. A hologram appeared in front of him. It was a video of all the most beautiful oceans from around the world. Everyone in the room was mesmerized.

As they watched, he continued:
"My name is Anael and I am the angel for the month of December. My favourite place in the world is anywhere where there is an ocean. I am classified as an angel of love and I think that love comes from deep within the ocean. Everyone, please put on your goggles for a minute."

Everyone obeyed him and within seconds they were all sitting on surf boards. It was the most beautiful day. A group of teenagers were either surfing or swimming. Anael said: "In my mind, it is this love that comes from deep within the water that draws people to the waves. I often sit in the ocean, close to where humans come to swim, just so that I can feel the weight of the world lift off their shoulders as they immerse themselves below the water." Everyone sat and took in all these great emotions. They could feel the joy, relief, and freedom of each of the teenagers at play. It was peaceful.

"This is why this particular child moved me so deeply." They were then transported to a home in a smaller town.

"It all started on a very hot day, way down south of Africa. This is AB's home town; they spend summers here and have been coming into the city for school terms so that AB and his brother could attend a good school. This happened when AB was just a small boy. I had been spending a lot of my time on this coastline because this part of the world is one of my favourite places during the month of December. The heat moves people towards the ocean, the air is perfect, and the sky is ever so blue.

There is a sense of excitement during the summer here; people are out and about, the days are long and the nights are enchanting. Early one morning as I flew over the waking town and I picked up that a tiny human was emitting large volumes of anxiety. I hadn't yet interacted with this little guy. The other children in the town seemed to be buzzing; something good was coming their way that day, so I didn't understand why this little guy was worried?

Mr Richards watched the family as they all sat around the breakfast table. The boy's brother was about 2 years older than him and he was chatting away to his mother while he ate breakfast "You know Mama, we each get a t-shirt and for lunch there are hotdogs. I hope that I am in a team with Ray. Mama, do you think there will be bluebottles on the sand today?" He scooped up another spoonful of his porridge and looked up at his mother. Mr Richards could tell what AB was thinking, and the thought of those "magical blue bottles" sent shockwaves of fear through him.

Mr Richards asked: "Why is he so worried?" Anael replied: "You see, today was the first day that he was going to see the ocean. It was the first day he was going to ride on a bus without his mother and his overactive imagination was filing him with dread."

The brothers got up to leave. Their mother waved at them from the doorway of their house. His brother took his hand and said, "Come on, we can't be late!" They ran hand in hand to the bus stop. When they got onto the bus, his brother left him with the other younger children and went to sit with the older boys at the back of the bus. Mr Richards and Anael sat on the bus with him; all the other angels were sitting on top of the bus, enjoying the ride.

The children were so excited; it was a day away from the dusty streets of their small town. Food, clothes, sun and fun were on the way. AB sat motionless as fear gripped him. His thoughts sounded something like this: What is the ocean? What are bluebottles? Will it hurt? What lives there? But I can't swim! The unknown was just too big.

As these thoughts consumed AB, Anael sat in front of him and softly blew sea air towards him; he wanted him to become familiar with the salty smell that he treasured so much. Perhaps if he felt familiar with it he would feel more comfortable when he arrived.

Anael took Mr Richards' hand and said, "I want to show you what the kids are getting up to today." Within seconds Mr Richards was in the sky. He was flying! He couldn't contain himself; he loved every second of feeling free and safe. They flew ahead of the bus.

As they approached the beach they could see a large group of adults congregating at the lifeguard house. Music was playing, food stalls were set up, and all along the beach there were what the humans called "cricket pitches".

"What are they doing?" Mr Richards shouted at Anael as they flew over the beach. "Today the adult humans are turning this odd sport called cricket into something spectacular, they are playing it on the magnificent sand and right next to the happiness of the ocean. They are giving the children of AB's small town the opportunity to have fun, learn a new sport and get a good meal." Anael sat Mr Richards down on the beach.

The buses began arriving. In total there were about 400 children on the beach that day. They were to get a snack, put on a t-shirt and line up with other children their age so that they could be put into teams for the morning. AB ignored all of this because as the bus was approaching the beach, he lifted his eyes and there it was … another world lay before him. Mr Richards could feel that the blue of the ocean was creeping into his veins and he began to feel it … he felt a deep connection to the ocean.

When the bus stopped, he climbed off and ignored everyone. He didn't want the snack, he didn't want the t-shirt, and he walked straight past the other children and ignored the adult voices that were commanding him to line up.

As everyone watched AB, Anael continued: "It was as if he was surfing a barrel and everyone around him was just a part of the barrel; the only end in sight was the ocean. He walked to the where the water could kiss his toes. His eyes had tripled in size and I could see that he was in love. All fear was washed away with the tide. It was the most beautiful thing that he had ever seen."

 Mr Richards stood next to him and it was if he was also seeing the ocean for the first time; he realised that he couldn't remember the first time he had seen the ocean. He had taken that for granted. It was truly spectacular.

A hand touched ABs shoulder and the trance was broken. He made his way to the other children; his worry was gone and he was free to enjoy the happiest day of his little existence thus far. Anael said: "I think that he will always be a child of the sea now. He will always look for her and use the power of the ocean to ease his worries. After he walked away, I surfed the nearest wave, happy to have been a part of his magical day."

08

Dora's
Snow
Story

Back in the classroom everyone was happier. Mackey-D was pouring out the sand from his shoes and Amy was fixing her wind-swept hair. Raguel said, "Isn't it amazing what the eyes of a child can see?"

"I am beginning to see." Mr Richards walked over to where AB sat and he noticed that in the margins of his work he had been doodling waves. He thought to himself that it truly was amazing how these memories had such an impact on them. Every day in the life of a child is special.

Mr Richards was getting used to how peculiar all the angels were. Their strange characteristics were endearing and he felt like he was getting to know them. One of the odder-looking angels stood up. He was dressed like a game ranger, and had even adopted a bit of an Australian accent. "Good day mate, the name is Hamaliel but you can call me H," he said, as he walked over to shake Mr Richards' hand. "Umm … good day, H."

Gabriel suddenly jumped up and hid behind his chair. He screamed, "Is there a lion nearby?" The other angels started to laugh.

"Give it a rest, Gabriel," said Raguel.

Hamaliel was a good sport; he giggled and continued, "Yes, yes, laugh as much as you want. Mr Richards I am dressed like this because one of my favourite things to do with my children, the children born in the month of August, is to accompany them when they travel the world."

"Why would you want to do that?" Mr Richards asked.

"Well, remember how you felt when AB walked up to the ocean for the first time?"

The feeling of euphoria and wonderment that Mr Richards had felt earlier washed over him; he smiled and nodded at H.

"That is what it is like travelling with a tiny human. Everything around them is new and for the most part, their emotions are incredible. Sometimes they get scared and overwhelmed but the curiosity of a child is often bigger than their fear, so they take everything in and enjoy it."

"I have many stories," H continued, "but there is a very sweet one about a girl in your class." He walked over to a shy looking girl and said: "Everyone, this here is Dora. She is an only child and she is quiet. She doesn't have too many friends and prefers to spend her time indoors, reading. Dora has an amazing imagination and she is often dreaming up new places. When she was younger she had watched a movie about penguins in the snow and for some reason she was drawn to it. She longed to experience it. She had only ever dreamt of snow.

"For years her dreams had been covered in white, snow fascinated her. It was only ever in her dreams though, because she came from a land so hot that even before snow was a thought in someone's mind, it was melting. This all changed when she went on a business trip with her father to a place up north for the winter. Let's join them there."

Everyone put on their goggles. When the room came into focus, Mr Richards noticed that they were in a hotel dining room. H was no longer dressed like a game ranger; he now looked like an Inuit. Gabriel came up to him and peered inside his hooded hat. "Polar bears anywhere?" he asked. H just chuckled again. "C'mon mate, leave us alone," he replied.

Dora was sitting at a table with four other adults. The adults were talking away and hadn't noticed her at all. It had been terribly cold for days. When her dad made her go outside, she moved with the speed of light because if she moved any slower she would freeze on the spot. She had spent the entire day indoors with her dad and these other adults. Mr Richards noticed a group of kids come in from outside; they were covered in snow and had big smiles on their faces. Dora noticed them straight away and her heart raced. She thought, "Snow, snow, snow! Can it be true?"

She peered over at them and tried to listen to their conversation as they ran over to their parents' table. There was absolute glee on their faces as they explained their morning to their mother.

"Mom, I fell so many times" one boy said with the biggest smile on his face "Dad, I built a snowman" or "Dad, we had had snowball fights" they said. She didn't understand their joy and happiness as she listened to them.

She had never seen snow, she had never touched it, and she did not know what a snowball felt like. This longing grew inside her, she needed to go outside; she needed to see the world covered in white.

She jumped up from the table and started to leave. As she did so, her father shouted, "Dora! Where do you think you are going?" She looked at him. Mr Richards could feel fear and sadness wash over her; she thought that her dad wouldn't let her go. She said to him, "Snow, Dad, snow. Please can we go look." Her dad sensed that this was important to her, so he politely excused himself. "Sorry gents, we are from the south and this is my little girl's first time seeing snow. I won't be too long." The other men at the table smiled and motioned for him to carry on.

"Let's go!" he said as he took her hand and led her to the hotel room so that she could get warm clothes. Mr Richards could feel her excitement grow. She put on layers and layers of clothing. As she walked outside, her spirit lifted. She could not contain her smile. She smiled from ear to ear as she ran towards the nearest pile of snow to touch the icy fluffiness for the first time. It was so soft and so cold. She looked around her and everything was white; the once dirty and dusty street was transformed into something new. It looked clean and full of promise; the biggest city that she had ever been in was suddenly magical.

When her father saw how happy she was, he completely forgot about the businessmen waiting for him inside. He took her for a walk and watched the snowflakes dance around her.

Every leaf that was left on the trees was hugged by the softest snow. As the leaves floated to the ground she could hear the slightest "poof" sound as they touched the ground below them. When she had dreamt of snow it was never as vivid as it was that night and even though she was freezing, the snow-covered city warmed her heart.

The scene faded to black. Mr Richards opened his eyes to see all the angels huddled together to get warm; they were showing each other the photos of the snow angels that they had made. They thought this was hilarious.

Mr Richards continued to watch them, and thought about the story that H had just shared. There was something different about this story. He realised that although Dora had felt extreme happiness, she hadn't learnt or overcome something like the other children had.

"Excuse me H, why did you tell me that story?" H was back in his safari suit and he began to grin from ear to ear. "I was secretly hoping you would ask."

This piqued the interest of the other angels so they began to listen.

"I told you earlier that Dora loves to read but did you know that Dora also loves to write?"

Mr Richards said, "No, I'm afraid that I didn't know that."

"Let me show you something quickly" H pulled out his aPad and a hologram appeared. It was of Mr Richards sitting at his desk. The rest of the children were doing some work. Dora came up to his desk. "What do you want?" Mr Richards barked at her, She plucked up the courage to hand him a piece of paper, and said, "I wrote this and I thought that maybe you would like it." Mr Richards didn't even look up from his desk as he replied, "Just leave it there; I will look at it later." Dora put the paper on his desk and sat down.

The hologram disappeared. Mr Richards had gone pale. "You never did read it, did you, Mr Richards?"

"No, I didn't."

"Well, it was a poem about her day in the snow and she just wanted someone to share it with. She thought that you might appreciate it, being a teacher. But you broke her heart, mate."

Mr Richards put his head in his hands and shook his head. "I didn't know."

"No, you didn't." H took off his hat and sat down.

09
I want to Ride my bicycle.

Raguel said: "As a child there are always lessons to be learnt. Some are harder than others but some are just pure fun! Azzie, don't you have a rather cute story about learning to ride a bike?"

"Oh yes!" she exclaimed. "That's most definitely one of my favourites." Mr Richards looked up from his hands and prayed that this story would make him feel better.

Azzie stood and began her story. "The name is Azzie, short for Asmodel and I am the angel for the month of April. I haven't laughed at a couple of kids this much in a very long time. When I replay this story in my mind I always wonder if the kids woke up that morning knowing that they were going to be so silly and create this fun memory for all of us. Sit back and let me tell you what happened that day to James and his sister." Everyone put on their goggles.

When everything came into focus, Mr Richards could tell that it was a crisp morning. You could feel that summer was ending and that winter was making her presence felt. They were outside someone's house.

Azzie spoke: "I was finishing up some business with a little guy who was suffering from some horrible nightmares, and as I was leaving his house I noticed a kid named James next door, he was riding around on his bicycle. I needed a break, so I sat in a sunny spot to watch him have some fun. His sister Mary came outside to play. She went to the garage to get her bicycle."

They watched the two of them. Mary's bike was a cute little blue bike that still had training wheels on it. She was riding around the driveway when she stopped to look at her brothers' bike. His was a very bright red, slightly bigger than hers, and it didn't have any training wheels on it. He noticed that she was no longer riding around, so he pulled up next to her: "What's up, sis?" he asked.

"Why does my bike have 4 wheels and yours only has 2?" "Well, because riding with 2 is more difficult and you are still little."

She was a stubborn kid and a day without a challenge for her was a waste of a day, so she said:
"Well, when can I ride with only two?"
A lightbulb went off in James' head, "Well, I suppose when you learn to do it…want to learn?"

Azzie froze the memory and turned to Mr Richards: "This is when alarm bells started going off in my head; they are both so young still. I thought 'How on earth was he going to teach her in a safe way?' I monitored their emotions, both seemed happy and unaware of the dangers that they were about to face."

"But why is this so dangerous? Mr Richards asked.

"Well, what I haven't told you yet is how their house was laid out. Let me draw it for you quickly. She took out what looked like a whiteboard marker but was able to draw in the air on it:

"There are 2 very steep hills on their property and the flat area in front of the house is very short. At the bottom of the second hill there is a wall. Is anyone else starting to see why I began to worry?"

Everyone inspected the surroundings. Mackey-D shouted: "Awesome!" and Vee just shook her head in worry.

Azzie continued, "In angel training we are taught that we cannot protect the tiny humans from everything and sometimes it is best just to let things play out. So, I took out my peanut butter and jam sandwiches and found a very good viewpoint to see what these crazy kids decided to do. I have packed a picnic for us."

Everyone sat under a tree and got comfortable. Peanut butter sandwiches and a flask of tea were passed around. Mr Richards was excited to try these peanut butter sandwiches!

Azzie unfroze the memory and Mary continued:
"Yes, I want to learn!"
"Ok, leave your bike here, we will use mine. Follow me."

They climbed up the first hill. When they were at the top he instructed her to sit on the bicycle. He ever so briefly explained about the brake system, the turning system and the pedals. She knew all this already because her little blue bike had them all … she was so excited. Her brown curls were blowing in the wind and she was ready to go. James held on to the bicycle and made sure that she was balanced, and, without warning, he let her go. Everyone's mouths dropped open, still full of peanut butter and jam sandwich. Everything slowed down….

Weeeeeee….
Off she went…
Her little hands held on so tightly to the handlebar…
She made it to the bottom of the first hill…
Her hair was blowing backwards…
She was miraculously balancing…
Her feet were flung off the pedals…
She was on the flat part still balancing as she made her way past the house…
It dawned on her, there was another hill… her eyes widened as she started going down the hill

...Oh my...

...A wall...

CRASH!!!

She went smack bang into the wall. They could hear James shouting, "Mary! Mary! Are you alright?" Mary was sprawled out on the grass with a silly grin on her face.

Azzie chimed in: "I used my scanner to check for injury but she had none. She was ecstatic." Mary looked like a cartoon character with little birds flying around the top of her head; her hair looked like it was their nest, and there were even little bits of grass sticking out of it. Everyone couldn't help but laugh. James fell down next to his sister and he too laughed and laughed and laughed.

Once they had stopped laughing at their own stupidity, James helped his sister up and dusted her off. He picked up his bicycle and said, "Wanna try again?" She merely replied "Okay" and they headed back up the hill.

"Oh boy, we are in for treat today," Said Anael.

Azzie continued: "You are indeed in for a treat, these two characters are very entertaining. They repeated their mistakes a few more times. Each time Mary went flying down the two hills, legs flailing about and her hair becoming wilder and wilder with every crash. My stomach hurt so much from laughing; these two children were relentless and fearless. Nothing was going to stop them from getting this right."

The angels and Mr Richards watched this amusing situation. After several attempts. Azzie froze the memory and said:

"After a few times racing down the rollercoaster that was her backyard, Mary was thinking a little clearer. She began to play with the brakes; you could see the light bulb switch on in her mind as she realised that as she hit the flat area in front of her house and tapped on the brakes, she could start to slow down and turn so that she missed the second hill.

Azzie restarted the memory. Everyone watched as Mary attempted this again. Her first time didn't quite work out and as she turned she reached the hill and tumbled down the hill sideways instead of riding down it. Again, there were fits of laughter.

"On her fifth try she finally got it right, and as she brought the bicycle to a standstill James came rushing over to her and gave her a big hug. She had done it! They were victorious and they had conquered the rollercoaster! I was so proud of those two, they just didn't give up, they learnt something new and they had a bucket load of fun doing it."

The angels packed up the sandwiches and started heading off. As the images faded, they heard James say to his sister, "Want to play with my skateboard now?"

10
Her Daily Angel

Mr Richards still had half of his peanut butter sandwich with him. He couldn't tell which was better, the sandwich or the donut. As he was finishing off the sandwich he remembered that peanut butter and jam sandwiches used to be one of his favourites as a child. He wondered why he didn't like them anymore. This started him thinking about the first time he rode a bike without training wheels; this memory eluded him and that saddened him.

His thoughts were interrupted by a very soft voice, and he looked up to see who was talking. Sitting there was a very plain angel. She looked shy. Mr Richards hadn't noticed her this entire time.

She had the most beautiful voice. She said softly, "I especially like stories about siblings. For the most part, it is a wonderful bond that they share. Raguel, would you mind if I told a story about a girl in this class?"

"Not at all."

She remained seated; her hands were placed on her knees and her wings were neatly tucked behind her. She looked at Mr Richards and said:

"My name is Muriel and I am the guardian angel of all children born in the month of June. I could tell you stories, oh so many stories about the children that I look after. I have every story under the sun: stories of bravery, stories of laughter, stories of friendship, and even some sad stories, but the story that I am about to tell you is a story of the love and loyalty that siblings share.

"I find that humans sometimes get lost in their day-to-day routines and they can forget that it is the smallest and simplest act of kindness that keeps the world turning. It was a particularly quiet evening for me and I was doing my rounds in a very suburban neighbourhood. One of my favourite little girls lived in this neighbourhood. Her smile always brightened my day."

Muriel pointed at a girl sitting next to Sally. "That is Kate; she has long blonde hair and bright blue eyes, the type that make the clearest of blue oceans jealous. She is blessed to have an older brother. He is strong, he is selfless, and he has one of the biggest hearts that I have had the pleasure of witnessing. So I decided to sit with her that evening as she fell asleep. Let's go and see."

As the darkness faded they were all in Kate's room. Muriel was sitting next to her and she repeated a night time rhyme that the angels chant as they sit with little ones who are asleep, it's a message of comfort: "And as you dream, it may seem that the world is a scary place. All around you is an amazing grace and tomorrow you shall be happy and safe." Her voice was truly mesmerizing. Mr Richards thought that the children born in the month of June were particularly lucky.

The angels and Mr Richards were quite content sitting in the warmth of the room, listening to Muriel sing. It was a cold morning; the sun had not yet graced the skies with her rays when their mother woke them from their peaceful sleep. She told them that she had to go to work early and they must get up. They must get ready. Their tiny eyes slowly opened. Mr Richards could feel a sadness wash over Kate. It was still dark outside, it was cold, and all she wanted was more time in her home and with her family.

When their mother dropped them at school it was still dark outside, but off they went to face the day ahead of them. The angels danced in front of Kate as she walked, to try and defrost the frozen ground. They didn't want her to slip and fall. Her smile was important to this world. This child had energy about her – when she was sad it radiated to others and infected them. Oh, but when she was happy it felt as if everything around her was brighter.

As they walked onto the school grounds, Kate noticed how dark it really was. Their school was on a large open property and the space between school buildings provided lots of room for shadows. There was a long tunnel which they had to walk through to get to the side of the school where they could stay warm until the sun blessed them and warmed their hearts. Mr Richards could feel the crippling fear take hold of her.

The two children stood side by side in front of the tunnel; it was the darkest tunnel they had ever seen. Kate looked up at her brother and as a tear rolled down her face, she said "I...I am scared." Her selfless brother warmly smiled at her and took her hand. Although he was also scared, he said to her, "Come on, I am here. I am always here. Let's do this together."

And so they did. Hand in hand they made their way through the tunnel. At the time it felt like the darkest and the longest tunnel they had ever walked through but there is something about feeling the warmth of another's hand in yours that is extremely comforting.

As the angels stood at the end of the tunnel and watched the two conquer their fear together, Muriel took Mr Richards' hand and said, "On this day, this boy made my job easy. You see, in the moment that he took her hand, he became her guardian angel. I could proudly spread my wings and fly into the sky. I was so happy because I knew that the blonde, blue-eyed happy girl would forever have a guardian angel and he took the form of her older brother."

11
The
Journey

The feeling of Muriel holding his hand lingered with Mr Richards for a while. He couldn't remember the last time he felt such genuine affection.

"Not all relatives and siblings are nice all of the time, though," a rather short angel said. He had a full beard and bald head. "I have seen some of the most horrendous fights between siblings."

"Yeah, me too" agreed Gabriel, "but there always seems to be something that the kids learn from it. Even if its years later."

"Sometimes," said the bald angel. "I often feel that fights with relatives or siblings mainly lead to regret"

"Do you have a story in mind?" asked Raguel.

"I do, in fact." He stood up and went over to a girl sitting at the front of the classroom. She was a foreign exchange student from China. "This little girl's name is Taotao. Did you know that, Mr Richards?"

Mr Richards looked confused "Sorry, did you say Taotao? I have always called her Ruby."

"Taotao is her real name; she chose an English name when she came to study here."

"Oh!" Mr Richards said, surprised. He had never bothered to ask, he had only assumed.

"Well yes, I would have guessed that you wouldn't know that. For reference, my name is Adnachiel but all my friends call me A.D. One frosty afternoon, I found myself in the eastern part of the world and I was playing around in the clouds above the Great Wall of China when my Halo started vibrating. Somewhere close there was the smallest cry for help. I fine-tuned my halo and it picked up fear, panic, and sadness. I set the location into my wings and set off. The quickening of this tiny human's heartbeat drew me closer to her at a rapid pace."

Everyone was putting on their goggles. In the memory, Mr Richards found himself in a place he had never seen before. The buildings were so tall; there were street vendors all around him, and people were hustling and bustling around on bicycles.

A.D. continued: "As I arrived, I blew her a kiss to send her a little comfort. For a moment her panic subsided. I stayed near to her to suss out the situation." Mr Richards noticed that shadows were starting to dance around the city as the last rays of the sun bounced off the large buildings and down below, in the city's veins, the children played in the chilly darkness.

There was a large group of children playing outside in the street that evening. The group was a mix of boys and girls and some were older than others. Taotao was the smallest of the lot and he could see an older girl talking to her. Every night they would meet outside to play.

"I searched my database of children and WingRing told me that the girl in distress was 6 years old at the time. The older girl she was talking to was her cousin, Liuliu. I flew around the two to listen to their conversation and create a feeling of warmth around them."

The older girl was growing angry and snapped: "You must go home!"

"B-b-but its dark, can't you come with me?" sniffled the younger one.

"No, I don't want to…just go already!"

The strangest thing happened to Mr Richards in that moment. He could hear that the two girls were speaking a language foreign to him yet he could understand every word they were saying.

A.D. addressed the group: "Turns out that Taotao was meant to be home earlier than her cousin but they normally walked home together. Today her cousin had decided to stay longer with the older kids and instructed Taotao to leave."

Mr Richards could feel Taotao's heart break. These emotions were truly new to her. It was her first taste of betrayal and her first taste of the fear of the unknown.

She turned to leave; they watched her survey the surrounding buildings. She was thinking: Which way was the safest? Which way was the quickest? Which way was home? She started to walk, slowly at first, she was still so unsure of her own footsteps. As her cousin stood to watch her leave, Mr Richards could sense a certain amount of sadness in her.

She knew she had done something wrong, but the words had been said and now she had to live with the consequences. She had to let her cousin walk her own journey. Taotao made her way through the maze of buildings. She kept close to the buildings for protection like a young buffalo stays near to its mother when it senses danger.

"As her angel, all I wanted to do was sweep her up into my wings, fly her home and see her smile. For when a child on earth smiles it sends tiny ripples of happiness that spread all around the world. However, I could not, so I flew just in front of her and gently sang a song that she loved. I let my presence be felt and made her feet feel less heavy than they were," A.D. said.

She was so brave; with every step a tear fell but she soldiered on. She walked past the street vendors, past the men playing cards and through the ever-darkening shadows. She knew that she could do it; all she needed was to get home.

She arrived at her apartment block and stood at the entrance. As she looked up at the 32 stories above her, her mother came out the door and embraced her.

While in the warmth of her mother's embrace the child reflected on her short journey and she was proud. She had conquered the darkness of her journey and she had conquered the darkness of her fears.

As they watched the mother and daughter turn to go inside, a movement behind a nearby trashcan caught their eye. It was her cousin.

"I had not realized that two children would grow up a little that day. It was only when I saw a look of relief on Liuliu's face that I knew that earlier, as she had watched her little cousin leave, she knew that she couldn't leave her to do it alone. She followed her home and each step of the way she whispered her apologies to her cousin's soul. When her cousin finally got home, she smiled; she too was proud. She turned to go play again and I flew past her and gently kissed her on her cheek. Those two children were left stronger and more independent that day, each their own angel and an angel to each other for life."

Everything faded to black.

12
Caught in the Act!

Mr Richards looked over at Ruby; he understood a bit more about her now. As he reflected, he realised that she was in fact independent. He had never seen her ask anyone for help. He was yet again taken aback by how these moments that seem so small could have such resounding effects.

Suddenly the rather stern looking angel stood up and addressed Raguel:

"Raguel I will tell my story now. I will not sugar-coat it. Put on your goggles, Mr Richards."

No one argued with him; it seemed easier to simply obey.

In the darkness, the angel approached Mr Richards and said: "My name is Barchiel and I am the angel for the children born in the month of October. I am also the angel of honesty. Please try not to disrupt my thought pattern once we are in the memory." Mr Richards nodded and followed him into the light.

They were standing in a living room. Mr Richards could smell that food had recently been cooked. Lying on the couches were a young boy and his father. All the angels were lined up against the wall of the living room, almost afraid to intervene. Barchiel froze the room and moved around it, almost like a detective, as he explained:

"The child in question is a small child. His name is Seth and he is approximately 6 years of age. He is 1.1 meters tall and he weighs around 22 kilograms. He has sandy blonde hair and blue eyes. I have heard others describe him as 'cute'. They have also said things like 'Oh, he is so precious,' and one particularly annoying one, 'Oh, those blue eyes. He is going to be a heartbreaker one day!' The child has an interesting character, he is friendly and kind. Seth is also particularly clever, and he is trying to figure out the world. He seems to be in a hurry to learn so he often pushes the boundaries to see how people react, or even to see how the world in general reacts. And even though his soul has a few war scars on it already, he is getting stronger every day.

"Why was I there?" Barchiel pointed to a photo on the TV stand; it was of a new-born baby. "You see, there was a new child in his family and the child in question wasn't adjusting very well to this. He would have sudden outbursts of anger and severe moments of sadness. It was the first time that he was experiencing the destructive emotion: jealousy. He needed to learn how to handle this and he needed to be calmed down. I often sat with him when he had an outburst and I would try to tell him the importance of honesty and the importance of talking to his parents.

Honesty comes in many forms. I told him that he should even be honest about how he is feeling. That's an entirely different presentation; let's move on to the story. It all started one Sunday afternoon. Seth and his family had just finished their Sunday lunch. Roast chicken, cauliflower with cheese sauce, peas, corn, roast potatoes and gravy. Seth was content." He unfroze the memory and everyone watched.

Seth and his father were playing Monopoly when their game was interrupted by the cries of Seth's little sister. His sister was a sickly child, so she took up a lot of her parents' attention. His father ran off to see what was wrong and when he came back he said, "My boy, we have to go to the shop. We can finish our game later; do you want to come along for the ride?" Grumpily, Seth rolled off the couch and, much like a sloth, he slinked his way to the car.

As Mr Richards sat with him in the car, he could tell that Seth felt disappointed and jealous. Mr Richards could hear Seth's thoughts and they went something like this: She is so small, how could she take up so much time? Why am I not enough for mom and dad?

When they arrived at the shop, Seth ran off to browse. The angel brigade followed him. He discovered his favourite aisle – the aisle that no parent escapes and no child leaves unhappy… the candy aisle! Barchiel froze the memory again and handed everyone a small piece of candy.

"In Seth's' country, they have a very cool piece of candy; it is a small block of bubble-gum called a "Chappie". The most interesting thing…"

POP!

A loud sound of bubble-gum popping came from Mackey-D; he had enthusiastically unwrapped the bubble-gum and was already chewing. He stopped what he was doing. Barchiel glared at him. Mackey-D hung his head in shame. "Sorry, Barchiel," he said sheepishly.

"Forgiven. As I was saying, the most interesting thing about the 'Chappie' is that inside the wrapper are fun facts. Seth was drawn to these sweets. He loved to read these fun facts and it was something he always did with his father because he wasn't able to read it fully by himself yet. Of course, he loved the sugar too." Barchiel unfroze the memory again.

Seth didn't want to ask his dad to buy the bubble-gum for him, so instead he secretly unwrapped it, placed the bubble-gum at the back of his mouth and put the wrapper in his pocket. Seth could feel his little heart race, he knew what he was doing was wrong. A fear crept over him: "What if I am caught?" he thought. His angry voice spoke to him and said: "hmm I don't care, I want this candy!" He ran outside to wait for his father.

When his father joined him, Seth said, "Dad, look what I found on the floor." He held out his hand and in it was the Chappie wrapper. "Will you read it to me?" "Sure thing, buddy," his dad replied, completely unaware of what Seth had done.

Barchiel stated: "Seth tried this little trick three more times after that and every time he felt more and more anxious about what he was doing. Everything was about to change because as we know my fellow agents, the truth always finds its way out."

The memory changed, and once more they saw Seth waiting outside the shop for his dad. When he held out his hand with the wrapper in it, his father grew curious. He wondered why there was always a wrapper on the floor outside. He knelt down besides his son and asked him where he had found it.

As Seth spoke to his father, his father noticed the candy at the back of his mouth. "Where did you get that?" he asked, the anger growing inside of him. Barchiel whispered to Seth, "Honesty is the best policy. Have the courage to speak the truth."

Seth was petrified, the gig was up. A hiding was surely on its way and he could see the anger and disappointment on his father's face.

"I t-t-took it from the shop," he whimpered.

"I can't believe this!" his father shouted. "Get in the car this instance and we will talk at home."

"The whole car drive home Seth sat in shame and in fear. Barchiel sat next to him and sprayed his can of Calmeeze. When they arrived home, Seth was sent to his bedroom and his father went off to talk to Seth's mother. The whole time his father was gone, Barchiel kept reminding Seth that it is always best to be honest about how you are feeling, but when his dad came back Seth had no time to speak. His Dad lay next to him on his bed, looking up at the ceiling with his hands raised up and he was playing with his hands as he spoke. This was one of Seth's favourite things to watch; his dad often did this at night when he told him bed time stories and it calmed him down.

His father said, "You know what you did was wrong, right?"
"Yes," he answered feebly.

"Seth, you can't go around doing things like that. I want you to remember that your mother and I love you very much. No matter what comes our way and how things change, you will always be our little boy. Next time you want to do something like read a Chappie paper together or finish our Monopoly game just let me know, okay?"

Seth rolled towards his Dad and hugged him. "Okay," he said. "But don't think you are getting away scot-free. First thing tomorrow morning you are going back to the shop.

You are paying for all the Chappies that you took, and you will say sorry to the owner. Is that understood?"

Everything faded to black.

Back in the classroom, Barchiel finished off by saying: "The next day Seth did go to the shop and he struggled through his apology and his feelings of guilt, but once all had been set right and his apologies had been made, the child felt lighter. He had grown even stronger. Why did I want to share this story with you? Well, it's simple really. We angels at the Tiny Human Protection Agency have a very busy job and we can't always be there for every child, so it is comforting to know that the oversized humans are capable of understanding their own children. They are capable of being their guardian angels when need be."

13
Tag Team

Mr Richards looked exhausted now. He had seen so much; he was starting to realise how these tiny humans in his class had so much to learn and that perhaps he wasn't teaching them well enough.

Raguel stood up and addressed everyone. "Thank you, angels, for taking the time to share these stories with Mr Richards. We are almost done, my friends. We have a very special story for you, Mr Richards; this story will take you into the lives of two people. Uriel and Barbiel, are you ready?"

Two angels stood up. Barbiel was a very wise looking angel, he wore a blue suit and had glasses and a greying beard. "I am ready. Good day, Mr Richards."

Then Uriel stood up and walked over to Mr Richards. She knelt in front of him and took his hands. "Do you know who I am?"

Mr Richards felt a familiar warmth with her. "I ... I'm sorry but I can't say that I do. You do make me feel strangely safe, though."

Uriel stood up and kissed his forehead. "Don't worry," she said, "most people forget their angels when they grow up. I am your angel, the angel for children born in the month of September."

Mr Richards looked at Uriel. It was a look of curiosity and wonder. "Have you been with me my whole life?"

"For most of it. You were a special child, Mr Richards. You were full of life. Do you remember what your favourite thing to do was?"

Mr Richards hadn't thought about himself as a child for a long time. He sat there and thought for a while. He closed his eyes and tried to remember. Why was this so difficult to do?

Finally, a light bulb went off in his head and images started flashing through his mind. He saw drawings everywhere. He could smell the art supplies in his room, and he remembered. "I loved to draw and paint," he said, surprised at himself.

"Yes! Do you still draw?" asked Uriel.

"No, never!" exclaimed Mr Richards. How odd, he thought to himself.

"Put on your goggles, Mr Richards and follow me."

He met Uriel in the darkness. When she came to him with the torch to lead the way, she said, "I hope this will help you, Bobby." Bobby! His first name was Robert and when he was growing up everyone called him Bobby. It made him feel strange and his name was ringing in his head. Bobby … Bobby … Bobby … Bobby …

As the room came into focus, he could hear someone shouting his name. He quickly realised that they were in his old school. They were in his old classroom. Mr Richards suddenly felt afraid. He didn't like this place.

He looked to see where the shouting was coming from, and there she stood in all her glory … Miss King. A ripple of fear went through Mr Richards. He hadn't thought about her in years. When his classmates were on the playground they used to sing: "Miss King, Miss King. She will make your bottom sting. Miss King, Miss King, what a scary scary thing!"

He looked around the classroom and there in the corner he saw himself sitting; he was drawing. His child-self looked up at Miss King as she shouted his name, and then stood to address her: "Yes, ma'am?"

"Are you drawing again, you insolent little critter?"

"I'm sorry, Miss King." For some reason, Mr Richards was feeling guilt and shame but he didn't understand why. Why could he not draw?

Miss King continued, "I told you before boy, there is no place in this world for drawings like yours! What do I have to do to get you to listen?"

Bobby was shaking and so too was Mr Richards. Miss King marched over to Bobby's desk. She picked up his art book and began to rip it to pieces!

"No!" cried Bobby. "Please, Miss King, please don't!" Tears were streaming down his face. Mr Richards rushed to try and help him but he couldn't touch her, she couldn't hear him. He too burst into tears as he watched Miss King dig into his school bag and tear up every drawing that he had.

Everything faded to black.

Mr Richards was sobbing as they walked through the darkness. Uriel took his hand and led him into another memory. Mr Richards dried his eyes and when everything came into focus he realized that he was in his old bedroom. He watched himself storm into the room and lie on the bed.

He was crying. He was also so angry. Uriel froze the memory at this point and said to him:

"I was sitting next to you the entire time. I tried to tell you that it was all going to be okay and that you should continue with your passion. Unfortunately, Miss King had really hurt your feelings and you had let anger get the best of you. It was at this point in your life that you shut the Tiny Humans Protection Agency out."

The memory unfroze and Bobby stood up. As the tears rolled down his face, he began to rip up all his drawings. He tore every art piece of his off the wall. As he was doing so, he kept repeating, "There is no place for drawings like yours in the world. There is no place for drawings like yours in the world." He threw away all his art supplies and collapsed in a heap of fury and tears on his bed. His passion was dead. All the angels circled around Mr Richards. They opened their wings and created a circle of light and warmth around him while he cried.

Everything faded to black. Uriel motioned for Mr Richards to join her and Barbiel on Mackey-D's favourite bench. "I'm sorry that you had to relive that, Bobby." He was still crying, and said, "Why did she do that? That wasn't fair." Barbiel replied, "This is what we are trying to show you, Sir. We are trying to show you that everyone has a part to play in a child's life but some people choose to do so in a negative way. I want to show you something else, are you ready to go again?"

Mr Richards tried to compose himself. He stood up. "Alright, let's go," he said. Barbiel lifted the lantern and led them away. When everything came into focus, Mr Richards saw that they were in a big dormitory. It looked like a big hall and its walls were lined with small beds. Everything was in shades of grey, and it was cold.

There was no one in the room except for a small girl. She sat on her bed, reading a book. They walked closer to her. Mr Richards noticed that she was reading a beautiful picture book and she seemed so content in her own world.

Barbiel told Mr Richards that the little girl was in fact Miss King. Mr Richards was shocked! She looked so helpless and friendly. She looked so innocent. "She was a very lonely child. She lived in an orphanage and because she was very clever, she didn't have many friends, so she would spend a lot of time all by herself. She only believed in the beautiful worlds that lived inside books. The only problem was that the headmistress of the school didn't approve of reading anything that wasn't a text book."

As Barbiel was about to continue, a rather stern looking woman entered the room and bellowed, "June King! What do you think you are doing? You are meant to be in the library completing your homework." Little June King was so afraid; Mr Richards felt more fear than he had done in his own classroom. June tried to hide the book but the headmistress was not stupid. "Bring me that book, you insolent little critter!" June King took the book over to her. She was so tiny. Mr Richards could feel all hope drain out of her. The headmistress grabbed her by the ear and dragged her kicking and screaming out of the room.

Everything faded to black.

14

Goodbye

Back in the classroom, everyone was silent. Mr Richards got up from his chair and started walking around the classroom. He was looking at each child. He began to see them differently. Each one was now a vessel of hope. Every child had their own world to deal with and he was a big part of it. He finally saw that he had to break the cycle. Children were important, and so too were teachers.

He looked at the angels; they were watching him closely. He addressed the group. "Thank you," he said. "Thank you for reminding me of whom I once was and thank you for showing me what my purpose is."

Raguel said, "We are sorry that we didn't intervene in Miss King's life sooner. This is now your task – it is your task to make sure that each day is special for each of these children. Without you, our job is particularly difficult."

All the angels stood up, and Raguel continued, "It's time for us to leave; there are many children out there that need us now. You know what you must do, Mr Richards."

"Yes," he replied.

The angels came to him and one at a time they said their goodbyes. Uriel hugged him and said, "I'm sorry that I couldn't help you more before, but if you ever need me, remember that I am always somewhere out there. Call to my Halo and I will be there."

The angels began to form a circle. They wrapped their wings around each other and bowed their heads. Raguel began to chant:

Are you Cherubim, the ones who proclaim defence of the little people?
Yes, yes, yes we are!
Are you their choir whose voices only carry messages of love? Yes, yes, yes we are!
Every day will you strive to comfort and protect?
Will you do so with passion and conviction?
Yes, yes, yes we will!
Make your pledge:
To you our little ones, we promise to put a smile on your faces,
We will be your light in the darkest of spaces,
We will be your warmth on the coldest of days,
We will guide you through any maze,
And through it all, we wish only to be your friend.
On us you can always depend.
To you our little ones, this is our solemn promise.

There was a flash of light, and they were all gone. The children began to move. Mr Richards said, "Ok class, pack up your books. It's time to leave."

The children were shocked; it had only been a minute since they started writing. "Before you leave everyone, I have some homework for you." A few groans came from the class. They thought they were going to have to finish their lines at home. But Mr Richards continued: "Tomorrow is show and tell. I want you to bring your favourite item from home and tell everyone about it." The class was shocked; they had never been allowed to bring anything from home. A ripple of excitement moved through the room. The children left the class feeling happy.

15

A Change

A few months had gone by, and Raguel was sitting on top of Mr Richards School once again. There were still twenty minutes until the school bell would ring, so he decided to pop in and see how Mr Richards was doing. He sent a message on WingRing to the group. It read:

Good day angels, please meet me in Mr Richards's classroom in two minutes – R

Mr Richards was busy reading a book to the class when Raguel walked in. This time, Mr Richards was not afraid of him. The class had frozen again and Mr Richards walked up to Raguel and shook his hand. "Welcome back," he said.

"I must say, it's good to be back." Within seconds the classroom was filled with light and all the angels appeared. Mr Richards was very happy to see them. They hugged or shook hands.

"The angels don't have long today, Bobby, but we just wanted to check in on you. What's new?" Raguel said.

"A lot has changed since your visit. Why don't you take a look around?"

The angels began to move around the classroom. Mr Richards had done a great job. There was a reading corner, where the children could sit together and read their favourite books. There was a family wall and it was covered with happy photos of everyone's families and even their pets!

There was an art corner and a favourite's wall, and the desks were no longer in orderly rows; they were now in groups. The classroom felt welcoming and warm. All the angels gathered around one particular wall. It was to be their favourite wall. It was a wall of birthdays, where each child wrote down their birth date. Each month of the year also had the name of the angel who took care of them! Mr Richards had drawn a cartoon picture of the angels. The detail was amazing. The angels were touched. "Good job, Bobby," Raguel said, "It's time for the angels to say their good byes. I don't think that you will need us again."

One by one the angels moved past Mr Richards and said farewell. Mr Richards felt saddened because he knew that he could never fully thank them for opening his eyes and his world to so much happiness. The angels could feel his gratitude, and no words were needed. Uriel merely said, "I am proud of you, Bobby," and she disappeared.

It was only Raguel left. Raguel asked Mr Richards if he would like to join him on the roof after the bell. "I would most certainly like that."

"Great, let the class know that you won't be here and come outside."

Raguel disappeared and the classroom unfroze. Mr Richards said to the class, "Alright everyone, I want you to go to the reading corner and choose a book. When the bell goes you can head home. I need to go somewhere quickly."

The class obeyed; they loved the reading corner and off they went. Mr Richards went to join Raguel.

As they were sitting on the roof, Mr Richards turned to Raguel and said, "Guess what?"

"What Bobby?" Raguel asked curiously.

"I've discovered that I actually do like ice cream."

"Fantastic!" Within and instant two ice cream sundaes appeared. They began to eat in silence. The school bell went and all the children came rushing out. Mr Richards felt an incredible wave of happiness wash over him. As they enjoyed that moment, Raguel saw Mr Richards' glowing expression. A tear rolled down Raguel's face.

Mr Richards looked at Raguel and said, "I still find you a rather peculiar man."

They laughed and ate another spoonful of ice cream.

Printed in the United States
By Bookmasters